NIKITA KUCHEROV
HOCKEY SUPERSTAR

BY RYAN WILLIAMSON

Copyright © 2020 by Press Room Editions. All rights reserved. No part of this book may be used or reproduced in any manner whatsoever, including internet usage, without written permission from the copyright owner, except in the case of brief quotations embodied in critical articles and reviews.

First Edition
First Printing, 2019

Book design by Jake Nordby
Cover design by Jake Nordby
Photographs ©: Del Mecum/Cal Sport Media/Zuma Wire/AP Images, cover, 1, back cover; Scott Audette/NHLI/National Hockey League/Getty Images, 4; Chris O'Meara/AP Images, 7; Mark LoMoglio/Icon Sportswire, 8, 21; marinat197/Shutterstock Images, 9; Thomas Eisenhuth/dpa/picture-alliance/Newscom, 10; Jeff McIntosh/The Canadian Press/AP Images, 13; Yuriy Kuzmin/AP Images, 15; Brad Rempel/Icon Sportswire, 16, 30; Keith Gillett/Icon Sportswire, 19; Jason Mowry/Icon Sportswire, 22; Julio Cortez/AP Images, 25; Paul Sancya/AP Images, 27; Red Line Editorial, 29

Press Box Books, an imprint of Press Room Editions.

Library of Congress Control Number: 2019936728

ISBN
978-1-63494-100-6 (library bound)
978-1-63494-109-9 (paperback)
978-1-63494-118-1 (epub)
978-1-63494-127-3 (hosted ebook)

Distributed by North Star Editions, Inc.
2207 Waters Drive
Mendota Heights, MN 55120
www.northstareditions.com

Printed in the United States of America

About the Author
Ryan Williamson is a sportswriter based in the Minneapolis–Saint Paul area. His articles have appeared in various publications across the United States. He lives with his miniature dachshund Minny.

TABLE OF CONTENTS

CHAPTER 1
An Impressive Debut 5

CHAPTER 2
Russian Star 11

CHAPTER 3
Making His Mark 17

CHAPTER 4
A Bolt of Success 23

Timeline • 28
At-a-Glance • 30
Glossary • 31
To Learn More • 32
Index • 32

1 AN IMPRESSIVE DEBUT

Nikita Kucherov battled for position in front of the net. A defender tried to keep him away, so Kucherov skated back a few paces. He was ready for a pass from his teammate.

Kucherov was playing in his first National Hockey League (NHL) game. He and the Tampa Bay Lightning were squaring off against the New York Rangers in November 2013. Two minutes into the first period, Kucherov had not yet taken a shot. But that was about to change.

Nikita Kucherov competes in his first game as a member of the Tampa Bay Lightning.

Kucherov's teammate passed the puck from the corner. As the puck approached, Kucherov wound up and blasted a powerful one-timer. The puck screamed through the air and bounced off the goalie's shoulder. Then it fell behind the goalie and trickled into the net. Kucherov pumped his fist as he skated toward his teammates to celebrate.

Kucherov's first career goal had come on his first shot as an NHL player. It was a sign of great things to come.

MORE HISTORY MADE

Nikita Kucherov's first NHL game was special for another reason. It was the 1,000th career game for Lightning teammate Martin St. Louis. The right winger was honored with gifts and a tribute video. After Kucherov's early goal, St. Louis scored the next two and added an assist in a winning effort.

Kucherov celebrates the first goal of his NHL career.

KUCHEROV'S FIRST GOAL

1. Kucherov skates away from a defender.

2. A teammate sends Kucherov a pass.

3. Kucherov blasts a one-timer into the net.

2 RUSSIAN STAR

Nikita Kucherov was born on June 17, 1993, in Maykop, Russia. Hockey was always a big part of his life. Growing up, his bedroom wall was covered with pictures of famous Russian players. Nikita started playing hockey when he was five years old. His family didn't have much money to spend on hockey equipment, but he thrived anyway.

When Nikita was seven years old, his father got a new job in South America. The family moved, but Nikita stayed in

Nikita Kucherov skates with the puck during the 2011 World Under-18 Championships.

Russia and lived with his grandmother. With the help of his hockey coach, Nikita continued to improve his skills. The two talked about hockey strategy. Nikita learned about different ways he could score goals. He also learned the importance of always moving while on the ice.

In 2011, Team Russia selected Nikita for the Under-18 World Championship in Dresden, Germany. Scouts from the Tampa Bay Lightning were on hand. They noticed how competitive Nikita was. They also saw how well he could react to what was happening on the ice. Nikita set a tournament record with 21 points in just seven games.

Nikita split his time between Russia's Minor Hockey League and the Kontinental Hockey League (KHL). The KHL is the top professional league in Russia. In June 2011, Tampa Bay

Kucherov (9) attempts a shot during the 2012 World Junior Championships.

selected the 18-year-old Kucherov in the second round of the NHL Entry Draft. Based on his ability, many experts believed Kucherov should have been taken sooner. However, teams worried that he wouldn't want to leave Russia to play in North America.

When Kucherov was drafted, he was dealing with a shoulder injury. He believed he needed surgery. His Russian team wasn't so sure. The team said he needed to pay for the surgery himself. With that in mind, Kucherov decided to talk to Tampa Bay. The Lightning agreed to pay for the surgery. But if they did, they expected him to play in North America. So, Kucherov made the move in 2012.

Kucherov wasn't ready for the NHL quite yet. In 2012, he played for the Quebec Remparts, a junior team in Canada. After a

A TASTE OF THE NHL

Nikita Kucherov did not experience an NHL game in person until 2013, when he was nearly 20 years old. He and his parents attended a playoff game between the New York Rangers and Washington Capitals. They were there to see fellow Russian Alexander Ovechkin, star left winger of the Caps. Three players on the ice that night—Ryan McDonagh, Dan Girardi, and Anton Stralman—ended up being Kucherov's teammates in Tampa Bay.

Kucherov scores the winning goal during a shootout at the 2013 World Junior Championships.

handful of games, the Rouyn-Noranda Huskies picked him up in a trade. Kucherov thrived, scoring 26 goals in 27 games. Kucherov's excellent season proved that he had what it took to play for the Lightning.

3 MAKING HIS MARK

Nikita Kucherov's NHL career started with a bang when he scored a goal on his first shot. But the rest of the 2013-14 season didn't quite live up to expectations. Kucherov ended up with only nine goals in 52 games as a rookie. Still, he showed signs of a player who could become great. For example, he could easily skate past defenders. He also created lots of scoring opportunities for himself and his teammates.

Kucherov prepares to make a move during a game in his rookie season.

Kucherov's first season with the Lightning may not have been amazing, but it got the attention of fellow Russian Pavel Bure. The right winger had played 12 seasons in the NHL. He believed Kucherov could be as great as other Russian stars such as Alexander Ovechkin.

Kucherov broke out during the 2014-15 season. Playing in all 82 games, he tallied 29 goals and 36 assists. Kucherov played on a line with Tyler Johnson and Ondrej Palat, two of Tampa Bay's best players. The three forwards

PLAYING FOR RUSSIA

Nikita Kucherov starred for Russia at the 2011 Under-18 World Championship. Since then, he has continued to play for his home country. In 2016, he played for Russia's senior team at the World Cup of Hockey. But his best tournament might have been in 2017. He had seven goals and eight assists at the World Championship that year. Through 2018, Kucherov had won three bronze medals and a silver medal while playing for Russia.

Kucherov attempts a shot during a 2014 game against the St. Louis Blues.

developed a good chemistry. They always seemed to know where the other players were on the ice. That awareness helped them make smart passes and set up scoring chances.

Kucherov also came through during the playoffs. In Game 1 of the second round,

Tampa Bay was on the road against the Montreal Canadiens. It was a tight contest, and the score was tied 1-1 at the end of the third period. During the second overtime, Lightning center Valtteri Filppula grabbed the puck along the boards. He zipped a pass to Kucherov, who was in the middle of the zone. Kucherov fired a rocket into the bottom corner of the net past the goalie's glove. Thanks to Kucherov's goal, Tampa Bay won 2-1.

In the next round of the playoffs, Kucherov scored again when it mattered most. In Game 3, the Lightning and the Rangers went to overtime tied 5-5. Tampa Bay forward J. T. Brown had just missed a breakaway attempt that would have given his team the win. But Kucherov made up for it shortly after when he ripped a shot into the net for the victory.

Kucherov's teammates swarm around him after his game-winning overtime goal against the New York Rangers.

Kucherov's two game-winning playoff goals helped Tampa Bay get all the way to the Stanley Cup Final. Unfortunately for Lightning fans, the team lost to the Chicago Blackhawks in six games. But Kucherov was emerging as one of the league's top young players.

4 A BOLT OF SUCCESS

After another successful season in 2015–16, Kucherov signed a three-year contract to stay with Tampa Bay. The following season, he finished with an impressive 85 points. He also played in his first NHL All-Star Game.

Because of injuries to teammates, Kucherov was often the guy Tampa Bay counted on to score. He did his part, racking up 40 goals. That was tied for second-best in the NHL. But the injuries proved to be too much for the Lightning.

Kucherov prepares to make a pass during a 2015 game against the Columbus Blue Jackets.

For the first time in Kucherov's career, Tampa Bay missed the playoffs.

Kucherov got off to a hot start in the 2017–18 season. He scored five goals in his first five games. And he didn't stop there. Kucherov went on to finish the season with 100 points. A big part of his success was that he had learned to read the game better. Lightning coach Jon Cooper said Kucherov knew what was going to happen before his opponents did.

Kucherov proved that in the playoffs. After a strong regular season, he scored five goals in the first round

PUTTING IN THE WORK

Nikita Kucherov scored 40 goals during the 2016–17 season. But he felt as if he should have scored more. So, Kucherov stayed in Tampa Bay after the season and worked with trainer Chris Ferazzoli. Three or four times a week, they practiced controlling the puck and shooting. Evidently, the practice paid off. The next season, Kucherov had 100 points for the first time in his career.

Kucherov shows off his stickwork against the New Jersey Devils during a 2018 playoff game.

against the New Jersey Devils. That helped him set a team record with 10 points in the series win.

The Lightning made it to the Eastern Conference Finals. But they came up a game short of the Stanley Cup Final. Alexander

Ovechkin and the Washington Capitals beat them in seven games.

In the 2018–19 season, Kucherov took his game to another level. His play helped Tampa Bay win 50 of its first 66 games. Kucherov broke the team's single-season points record when he notched his 109th point against the Detroit Red Wings. He went on to finish the season with a league-leading 128 points. That was the most points ever for a Russian player.

Thanks in large part to Kucherov, Tampa Bay finished the regular season with the best record in the NHL. Hockey experts expected the team to go far in the playoffs. Unfortunately for Kucherov and the Lightning, things didn't work out that way. In the first round, the Columbus Blue Jackets stunned Tampa Bay with a four-game sweep.

Kucherov scores against the Detroit Red Wings during a 2019 game.

Despite the tough loss, the 2018–19 season proved that Kucherov was one of the top stars in the game. In June 2019, he won the Hart Memorial Trophy, which is given to the league's most valuable player.

TIMELINE

1. **Maykop, Russia (June 17, 1993)**
   Nikita Kucherov is born in Russia and stays there until he is 18 years old.

2. **Dresden, Germany (April 2011)**
   Nikita plays for Russia in the Under-18 World Championship. He leads the tournament with 11 goals.

3. **Saint Paul, Minnesota (June 25, 2011)**
   The Tampa Bay Lightning select Kucherov in the second round of the 2011 NHL Entry Draft.

4. **Rouyn-Noranda, Quebec (November 2012)**
   In his first season of hockey in North America, Kucherov scores 26 goals in 27 games for the Rouyn-Noranda Huskies, a Canadian junior team.

5. **Tampa, Florida (November 25, 2013)**
   Kucherov makes his NHL debut with the Lightning. He scores a goal on his first career shot.

6. **Los Angeles, California (January 29, 2017)**
   Kucherov plays in his first NHL All-Star Game.

7. **Montreal, Quebec (April 7, 2017)**
   Kucherov scores his 40th goal of the season for the Lightning. It's the first time in his career he has scored 40 goals.

8. **Raleigh, North Carolina (March 21, 2019)**
   Kucherov becomes the first player to score 120 points in a season since 1996–97.

MAP

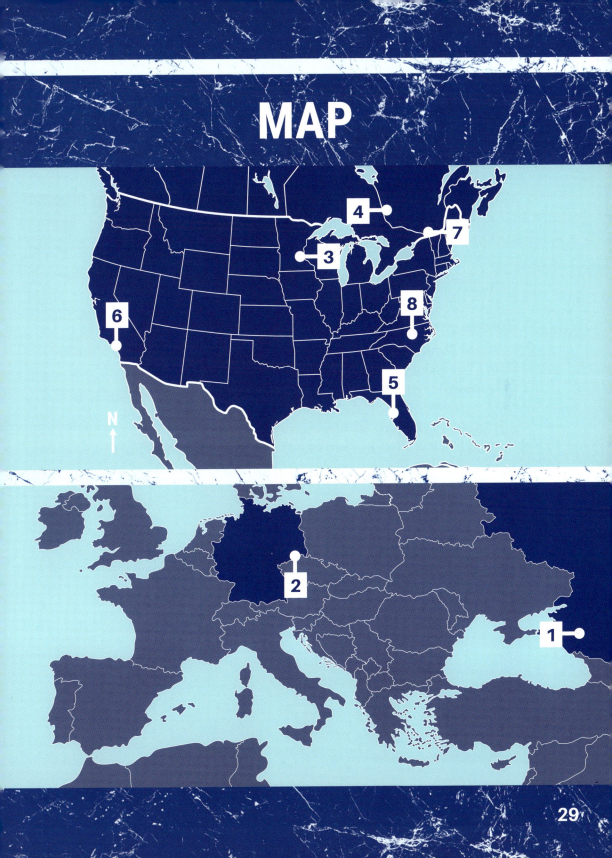

29

AT-A-GLANCE

Birth date: June 17, 1993

Birthplace: Maykop, Russia

Position: Right wing

Shoots: Left

Size: 5 feet 11 inches, 178 pounds

NHL team: Tampa Bay Lightning (2013–)

Previous teams: Rouyn-Noranda Huskies (2012–13), Quebec Remparts (2012), CSKA Moscow (2010–12)

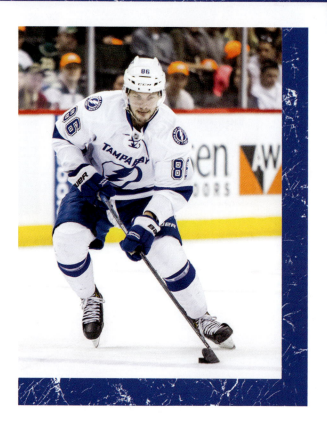

Major awards: Hart Mcmorial Trophy (2019), Art Ross Trophy (2019), NHL All-Star (2017, 2018, 2019)

Accurate through the 2018–19 season.

GLOSSARY

assist
A pass that results in a goal.

breakaway
When a player has a clear path to the net with no defenders between him and the goalie.

contract
A written agreement that keeps a player with a team for a certain amount of time.

debut
First appearance.

draft
An event that allows teams to choose new players coming into the league.

emerge
To become prominent or more well-known.

one-timer
When a player shoots a puck off his stick from a pass without stopping it.

playoffs
A set of games to decide a league's champion.

point
A statistic that a player earns by scoring a goal or having an assist.

scout
A person who looks for talented young players.

sweep
When a team wins all the games in a series.

TO LEARN MORE

Books
McCabe, Matthew. *It's Great to Be a Fan in Florida*. Lake Elmo, MN: Focus Readers, 2019.

Peters, Chris. *Hockey Season Ticket: The Ultimate Fan Guide*. Mendota Heights, MN: Press Box Books, 2019.

Peters, Chris. *Hockey's New Wave: The Young Superstars Taking Over the Game*. Mendota Heights, MN: Press Box Books, 2019.

Websites
NHL Official Site
https://www.nhl.com/

Nikita Kucherov Career Stats
https://www.hockey-reference.com/players/k/kucheni01.html

Tampa Bay Lightning Official Site
https://www.nhl.com/lightning

INDEX

Chicago Blackhawks, 21
Columbus Blue Jackets, 26

Detroit Red Wings, 26

Kontinental Hockey League, 12

Maykop, Russia, 11
Montreal Canadiens, 20

New York Rangers, 5, 14, 20
NHL Entry Draft, 13

Ovechkin, Alexander, 14, 18, 25–26

Quebec Remparts, 14

Rouyn-Noranda Huskies, 15

World Championship, 12, 18